BIG CHICKENS
GO TO TOWN

LESLIE HELAKOSKI ✽ illustrated by HENRY COLE

DUTTON CHILDREN'S BOOKS | AN IMPRINT OF PENGUIN GROUP (USA) INC.

DUTTON CHILDREN'S BOOKS

A DIVISION OF PENGUIN YOUNG READERS GROUP

PUBLISHED BY THE PENGUIN GROUP

Penguin Group (USA) Inc., 375 Hudson Street, New York, New York 10014,

U.S.A. ❀ Penguin Group (Canada), 90 Eglinton Avenue East, Suite 700,

Toronto, Ontario M4P 2Y3, Canada (a division of Pearson Penguin Canada Inc.)

❀ Penguin Books Ltd, 80 Strand, London WC2R 0RL, England ❀ Penguin

Ireland, 25 St Stephen's Green, Dublin 2, Ireland (a division of Penguin Books Ltd)

❀ Penguin Group (Australia), 250 Camberwell Road, Camberwell, Victoria 3124,

Australia (a division of Pearson Australia Group Pty Ltd) ❀ Penguin Books India

Pvt Ltd, 11 Community Centre, Panchsheel Park, New Delhi —110 017, India ❀

Penguin Group (NZ), 67 Apollo Drive, Rosedale, North Shore 0632, New Zealand

(a division of Pearson New Zealand Ltd) ❀ Penguin Books (South Africa) (Pty)

Ltd, 24 Sturdee Avenue, Rosebank, Johannesburg 2196, South Africa ❀ Penguin

Books Ltd, Registered Offices: 80 Strand, London WC2R 0RL, England

CIP Data is available.

Published in the United States by Dutton Children's Books,

a division of Penguin Young Readers Group

345 Hudson Street, New York, New York 10014

www.penguin.com/youngreaders

DESIGNED BY HEATHER WOOD

Manufactured in China / First Edition

ISBN 978-0-525-42162-7

10 9 8 7 6 5 4 3 2 1

To Ward,
for dancing and believing
— L . H .

To all of my
fellow fowl fans
out there
— H . C .

ONE SUNNY DAY four big chickens found a bag of chicken feed in the back of the farmer's pickup truck. They picked, pecked, and poked at the bag trying to get it open, when suddenly, the farmer started up the truck and drove away from the farm.

Four petrified chickens peeked out the back of the truck.

"Uh-oh," said the chickens, looking around, "this doesn't look like our farm."

"What if we never get home again?"

"What if we fall out of the truck?"

"What if we can't get this bag open?"

The lily-livered chickens shivered and quivered.

Lumpy tires whumped.
Hidden cargo thumped.
  Feed sack busted. Tailgate
rusted.
  Grain spilled. Cheeks filled.
  Eyes crossed until at last . . .

. . . the truck tossed the chickens out, and they plopped safely to the ground.

Four pummeled chickens followed the trail of feed to find —a strange street.

"Uh-oh," said the chickens. "This doesn't look like the road on our farm."

"What if we can't get across?"

"What if we get separated?"

"What if we get flattened?"

The chickens bawled, squalled, and caterwauled.

Craning necks curved. Rushing traffic swerved.

Gullets wheezed. Bodies squeezed.

Horns honked. Heads bonked. Toes scritched until at last . . .

. . . the light switched colors, and the chickens crossed the street.

Four peckish chickens followed the trail of feed to find—a strange smell.

"Uh-oh," said the chickens. "This doesn't smell like the food on our farm."

"What if we don't like it?"

"What if we can't swallow it?"

"What if we throw up?"

The chickens retched, stretched, and kvetched.

Bustling waiters tripped. Sidewalk tables flipped.

Chickens stewed. Napkins shooed.

Food swirled. Legs twirled. Mouths flopped until at last...

... food dropped into the chickens' mouths, and they ate every crumb they could find.

Four persnickety chickens followed the trail of feed to find —a strange noise.

"Uh-oh," said the chickens. "This doesn't sound like any noise on our farm."

"What if our eardrums burst?"

"What if our brains turn into mush?"

"What if we shake something loose?"

The chickens jerked, quirked, and berserked.

Twitching toes twiddled. Flying fingers fiddled.

Gizzards rocked. Eyebrows cocked.

Feet jammed. Chords slammed. Notes played until at last . . .

. . . chickens swayed, and they danced until they wore themselves out.

Four pooped chickens followed the trail of feed to find—a group of strange animals.

"Uh-oh," said the chickens. "These don't look like any animals on our farm."

"What if they don't like us?"

"What if they're mean?"

"What if they eat all the food?"

The chickens blabbered, gabbered, and gibber-jabbered.

Shouting voices wobbled.
Flighty locals bobbled.
  Running feet flumped. Startled
bellies bumped.
  Crowds rushed. Toes crushed.
  Hearts stuttered until at
last . . .

...wings fluttered, and the chickens followed the pigeons to safety.

Four plucky chickens looked around and sighed.

"What are we going to do now?" asked the chickens.

"We're lost."

"We're tired."

"We're hungry."

"It doesn't look like we'll ever get home."

The trail was gone. The chickens huddled together.

The sky grew dark. The chickens cuddled closer.

The pigeons flew away, and the befuddled chickens looked around to find . . .

. . . themselves standing on an empty feed bag in the back of the farmer's pickup truck.

"We're saved!" cried the chickens. The chickens skipped, tripped, and flipped. They flopped, dropped, and plopped. They laughed, cried, and deeply sighed.

"We can go home now," said the chickens, and they settled down in the truck.

"The city is full of strange noise."

"The city is full of strange food."

"The city is full of very strange animals."

"Yes," said the chickens. "Maybe we can come back again soon."

And four pummeled, peckish, persnickity, pooped, plucky chickens slept peacefully all the way home.